Billy & Milly Short & Silly

Written by
EVE B. FELDMAN

Pictures by
TUESDAY MOURNING

G. P. PUTNAM'S SONS

Stoops

Hoops

Scoops

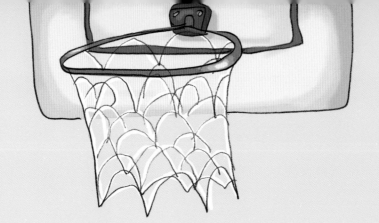

Oops

Dock

Rock

Shock

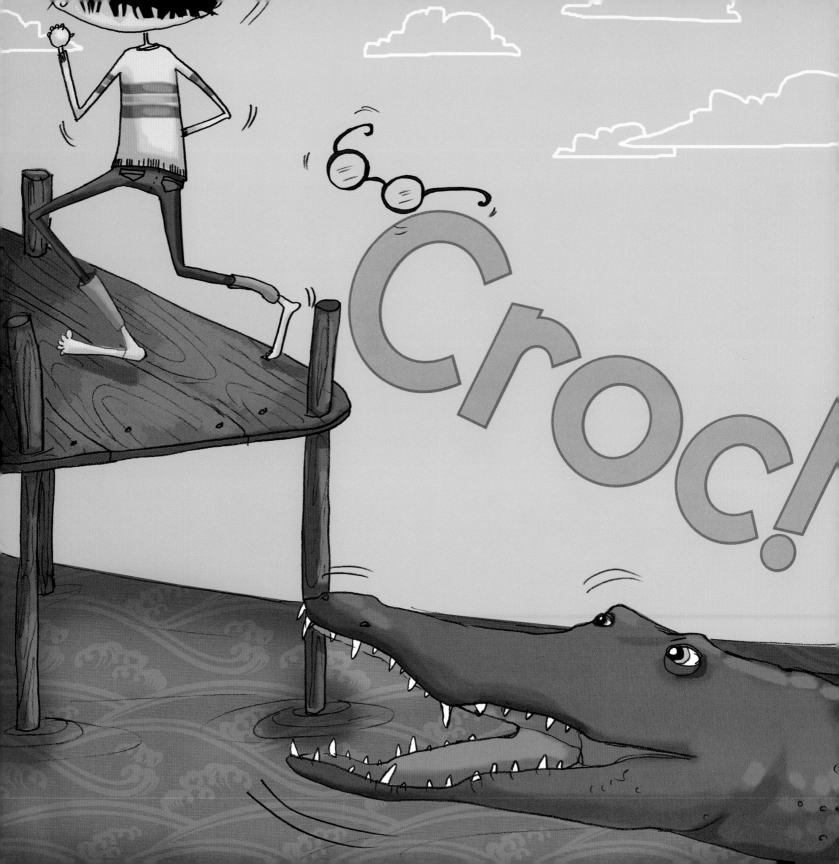

Cape

Bike

Spike

Hike

Gnat

Hat

Dream

Beam

Pack

WHACK!

Tee

Tree

Bee

Flee

Flame

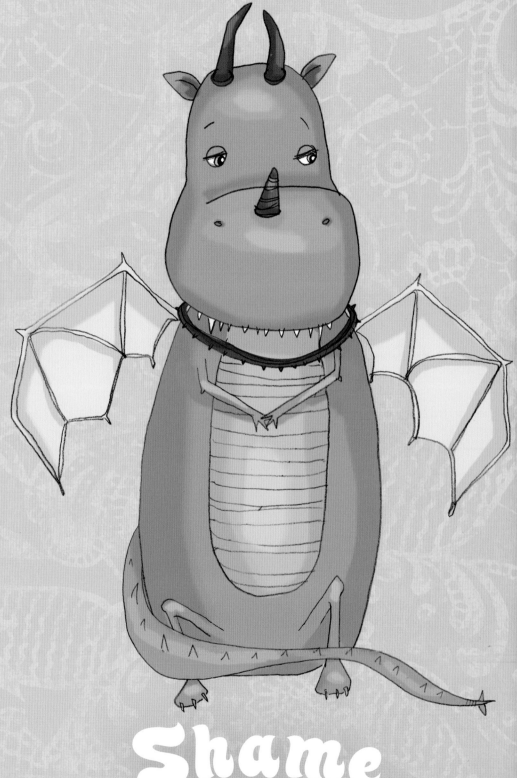

Blame

Shame

Tame

Room

Broom

Bunk

Trunk

Skunk

Clunk

Cow

Now...

WOW!

Bow

Shop   **Drop**

Mop

Flop

For Sophie Noa Feldman,
who loves stories
— E.B.F.

A big thanks to
J.D.L., A.J.L. and S.K.A.
— T.M.

G. P. PUTNAM'S SONS

A division of Penguin Young Readers Group. Published by The Penguin Group. Penguin Group (USA) Inc., 375 Hudson Street, New York, NY 10014, U.S.A.

Penguin Group (Canada), 90 Eglinton Avenue East, Suite 700, Toronto, Ontario M4P 2Y3, Canada (a division of Pearson Penguin Canada Inc.).

Penguin Books Ltd, 80 Strand, London WC2R 0RL, England.

Penguin Ireland, 25 St. Stephen's Green, Dublin 2, Ireland (a division of Penguin Books Ltd.).

Penguin Group (Australia), 250 Camberwell Road, Camberwell, Victoria 3124, Australia (a division of Pearson Australia Group Pty Ltd).

Penguin Books India Pvt Ltd, 11 Community Centre, Panchsheel Park, New Delhi – 110 017, India.

Penguin Group (NZ), 67 Apollo Drive, Rosedale, North Shore 0632, New Zealand (a division of Pearson New Zealand Ltd).

Penguin Books (South Africa) (Pty) Ltd, 24 Sturdee Avenue, Rosebank, Johannesburg 2196, South Africa.

Penguin Books Ltd, Registered Offices: 80 Strand, London WC2R 0RL, England.

Manufactured in China by South China Printing Co. Ltd.

Design by Marikka Tamura. The art was done in mixed media collage.

Library of Congress Cataloging-in-Publication Data

Feldman, Eve. Billy and Milly, short and silly / Eve B. Feldman ; illustrated by Tuesday Mourning. p. cm.

Summary: Relates the adventures of Billy and Milly in very brief, rhyming text and illustrations. [1. Stories in rhyme.]

I. Mourning, Tuesday, ill. II. Title. PZ8.3.F364Bi 2009 [E]—dc22 2008026143 ISBN 978-0-399-24651-7

1 3 5 7 9 10 8 6 4 2